A Prize for Percival

Library of Congress Cataloging-in-Publication Data

Langoulant, Allan.
    A prize for percival.

    Summary: Though people tell Prudence Penelope Potter
her pig Percival is not a proper pet, she enters him in the
Pet Parade anyway, hoping he will win a prize for the
Most Perfect Pet.
    [1. Pigs—Fiction. 2. Pets—Fiction] I. Title.
    PZ7.L269Pr 1988 [E]   88-42912
    ISBN 1-55532-931-4

North American edition first published in 1989 by

Gareth Stevens Children's Books
7317 West Green Tree Road
Milwaukee, Wisconsin 53223, USA

This US edition copyright © 1989
Text and illustrations copyright © Allan Langoulant, 1988
First published in Australia by Viking Kestrel,
Penguin Books Australia Ltd.

2 3 4 5 6 7 8 9 93 92 91 90 89

A Prize for Percival

Gareth Stevens Children's Books
Milwaukee

Prudence Penelope Potter had a pet pig.

The pig's name was Percival.

Some people told Prudence Penelope Potter
that a pig was smelly and dirty
and not at all a proper pet.

But Prudence Penelope Potter
loved her pet pig and, anyway,
she thought some people
were pretty smelly and dirty themselves.

Prudence Penelope Potter
read of a big Pet Parade
with a prize for the Most Perfect Pet.
She decided she would enter Percival.
Some people laughed.

But Prudence Penelope Potter didn't care.
She scrubbed Percival,
sprayed him with perfume,
and prepared him
for the Pet Parade.

On the day of the Pet Parade,
children came from near and far . . .

PET PARADE

. . . with just about every kind of pet
you could think of.

Just after the parade started,
a pet mouse got loose.

Pussycats pounced, dogs darted,
ducks dived. Fur and feathers
flew furiously, as all the pets
plunged into pursuit.
All, that is, except one.

The Pet Parade was pure pandemonium.

But Percival, the polite pig, sat peacefully.

The president presented Percival
with the prize for the Most Perfect Pet.

Prudence Penelope Potter was so pleased,
she hugged and hugged Percival.

The proud pair pirouetted, pranced prettily

and promenaded . . . all the way home.

And never again did anybody
tell Prudence Penelope Potter
that a pig was not a proper pet.

28

Which only goes to prove,
politeness pays.